# A Hippo
# in Our Yard

# A Hippo in Our Yard

## Liza Donnelly

I Like to Read®

HOLIDAY HOUSE • NEW YORK

Mom, we have a hippo
in our yard.

I don't think so, dear.

I will give it
some lettuce.

Here you go, Miss Hippo.

Maybe later.

I will give it some tuna.

Here you go, Mr. Tiger.

Liz, we have
zebras
in our garage!
We do!
Come see!

Not now. Go away.
I am texting Patty.

I will give them some carrots.

Here you go, zebra family!

Nana, we have koalas in our hammock!

That's nice, dear.

Want to see?

No, I believe you.
It sounds fun.
You can give them
some grapes.

Everyone
stay inside!
The zoo animals
got out!

Where is Sally?

For Ella and Gretchen

I LIKE TO READ is a registered trademark of Holiday House Publishing, Inc.
Copyright © 2016 by Liza Donnelly
All Rights Reserved
HOLIDAY HOUSE is registered in the U.S. Patent and Trademark Office.
Printed and Bound in April 2017 at Tien Wah Press, Johor Bahru, Johor, Malaysia.
The artwork was created with pen and ink and watercolors.
www.holidayhouse.com
First Edition
3 5 7 9 10 8 6 4 2

Library of Congress Cataloging-in-Publication Data

Donnelly, Liza, author, illustrator.
A hippo in our yard / Liza Donnelly. — First edition.
     pages cm.
Summary: "Sally tries to tell her family that a hippo, a tiger, zebras
and koalas are in their yard, but no one pays attention until they
hear that the zoo animals have escaped; now everyone panics
except for Sally!"— Provided by publisher.
ISBN 978-0-8234-3564-7 (hardcover)
[1. Zoo animals—Fiction.]  I. Title.
PZ7.D7195Hi 2016
[E]—dc23
2015022328

ISBN 978-0-8234-3844-0 (paperback)